Abney and Teal, how does it feel,
To live in the park on an island?
It's just right for us – it's adventurous!
And it's home, home on our island.

The Adventures of
ABNEY & TEAL

The More-Maker

Joel Stewart

WALKER BOOKS
AND SUBSIDIARIES
LONDON • BOSTON • SYDNEY • AUCKLAND

It's a bright, early morning in the park,
just right for everything to sparkle.
Teal is having a wash.
Abney is watering his sunflowers and
humming a little tune to help them grow.

Tum
te tum

Tra la la...

Drops of water glisten on the flowers in the morning sun. And, nestled amongst them, something else is gleaming brightly. "Teal," calls Abney. "I think you'd better come and look at this."

"What is it, Abney?" asks Teal.
"I think ... I think a bit of the sun
has broken off!" says Abney.

Nobody has ever seen the sun on the ground before! The Poc-Pocs begin to hop and chirrup excitedly.

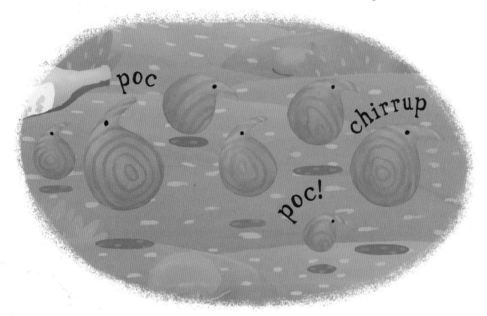

Neep pops out of his tunnel.

And they all gather round to look at the piece of broken sun.

"I wonder how it could have broken off," says Abney.
"I wonder how we can get it back up in the
sky again," says Teal.
"Perhaps we should just pick it up and throw it?"
"Ooh, be careful, Teal!" says Abney. "You might
burn yourself."

"Hmm, well let's look for something else to pick it up with," suggests Teal. "Come on!"

Neep finds two sticks, but the sun
keeps slipping out of them.

Teal tries with her umbrella, but it doesn't work.

"Look!" calls Abney. "I found this old tennis racket on my shelves and a long stick. Maybe we can use these?"
"Brilliant idea, Abney!" says Teal.

They push the piece of sun onto the
tennis racket with the stick.
"Ready? Steady?" calls Abney. "Go!"
The piece of sun flies up into the air ...

... and lands again just by the lake.

"Look!" says Teal. "It's not shining any more!"

"Well, the big sun has gone behind a cloud, so this piece of sun has stopped shining too," explains Abney.

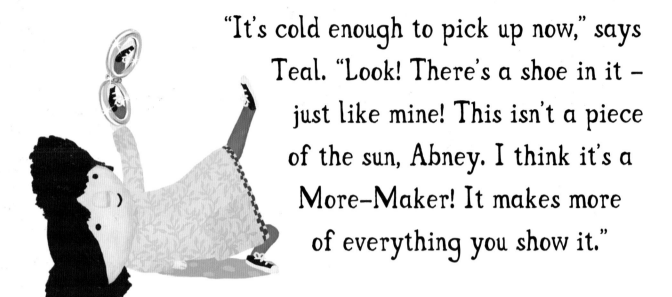

"It's cold enough to pick up now," says Teal. "Look! There's a shoe in it – just like mine! This isn't a piece of the sun, Abney. I think it's a More-Maker! It makes more of everything you show it."

"Let me see," says Abney. Sure enough, in the More-Maker he sees more of Abney!

"Oh!" says Abney, jumping back.
"That gave me a surprise!"
"Can I have a turn?" laughs Teal. She makes
funny faces into the More-Maker.

Ha ha!
More silly
faces!

Everyone wants to play with the More-Maker. The Poc-Pocs have a go...

More!

poc

poc

poc-poc!

Neep
has a go...

More
Neep!

Neep!
Neep!

"I know!" shouts Abney. "If the More-Maker can make more of everything, why don't we show it our porridge? Then we'll get more porridge!"
"Good idea," laughs Teal.
So Abney makes some porridge.

Tum te tum...

Yay, porridge!

"It's ready, Teal," says Abney.
"Let's show it to the More-Maker
and make – some – MORE!"

But the spoon just knocks against the More-Maker and the porridge won't come out. Teal is disappointed. "Abney," she says, "this More-Maker doesn't work after all."

"Well maybe the More-Maker doesn't really make more of everything," suggests Abney. "Maybe it just shows you what you've already got."

"You're right," says Teal. A smile spreads across her face. "And look, what we've got is just enough porridge for everyone!" "Hurray!" says Abney. "That was an adventure, wasn't it?"

The Adventures of ABNEY & TEAL

Other books from Abney and Teal:

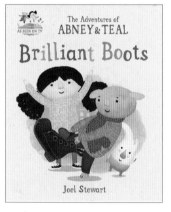

ISBN 978-1-4063-4490-5

ISBN 978-1-4063-4421-9

ISBN 978-1-4063-4491-2

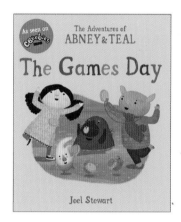

ISBN 978-1-4063-4811-8

Abney and Teal toys also available:

ABNEY & TEAL MIX & MATCH CARD GAME

ABNEY & TEAL BEAN TOY ASSORTMENT

ABNEY & TEAL 24 PIECE FLOOR PUZZLE

ABNEY & TEAL WOODEN DOMINOES

ABNEY RAG DOLL

TEAL RAG DOLL

TALKING NEEP PLUSH